This Book

<u>DEDICATION:</u>

To My Beautifully Crowned Princess and Prince,

Khariana and Athan, plus all of our friends!

My Curly, Coily Crown

By: Darcel Craft

Welcome, Reader!

*A **<u>SelfLove Seed</u>** is about to be planted!*

Take good care of it.

Water it often with kind words.

Give it lots of Sunlight.

And watch love grow.

-DarcelBeing

My Father is a KING,
He gave ME a CROWN!

It DEFIES gravity,
I don't hold MY HEAD down!

My FATHER is a KING,
He GAVE me a crown!

It GROWS UP to the sky,
And OUT, all around!

My Father is a KING,
He CROWNED me with CURLS!

I wear BRAIDS, twists, and PUFFS,
With ribbons that TWIRL!

My Father is a KING,
He CROWNED me with CURLS!

They LOOK just like my MOMMY'S,
When she was a GIRL!

My Father is a KING,
He CROWNED me with COILS!

They LOVE to drink WATER,
And great-smelling OILS!

My Father is a KING,
He CROWNED me with COILS!

I'm PROUD of my ROOTS,
They tell me I'm ROYAL.

My Father is a KING,
He CROWNED me with KINKS!

They have SUPERPOWERS,
To STRETCH and to SHRINK!

My Father is a KING,
He CROWNED me with KINKS!

Like the ANCIENT EGYPTIANS,
My styles are unique!

Now Do you SEE,
your HAIR Is ONE-of-a-Kind?

BEAUTIFULLY Made,
So THICK and DIVINE!

Your CURLY, COILY crown is
custom-made from ABOVE,

YOUR Father is a KING,
So He CROWNED YOU, with LOVE!

THE END

Now It's Your Turn!
List 5 things you like about
Your Hair:

1. _____ !

2. _____ !

3. _____ !

4. _____ !

5. _____ !

Thank You For Sowing This _SelfLove_ Seed!

Contact Me:

Email: _darcelbeingbooks@gmail.com_

Visit Me:

www.darcelbeingbooks.com

Follow Me:

IG: @darcelbeingbooks

Made in the USA
San Bernardino, CA
14 November 2018